PACHAMAMA TALES

S.C. Haas

Pachamama Tales

Copyright © 2017 by S.C. Haas
Revised May 2017

All rights reserved.

Stories, design, and illustrations by S.C. Haas

Reader views on Amazon are always appreciated; please send comments to **schaas@gmail.com**.

PREFACE

While Earth Mother Pachamama is of Andean
origin, she is present in many indigenous religions.
I first learned of her on a trip to Machu Picchu in
Peru.

To me, she epitomizes the goodness and caring of a
benevolent being, intrinsically tied to the natural
world and its creatures.

"Pachamama Tales" are graphic presentations of her
stories. Some are based on the belief systems of
indigenous peoples throughout the Americas, others
are the imaginings of the author. All serve to
describe the wisdom of Pachamama.

PROLOGUE

Pachamama is concerned about how we treat each other and how we humans steward the earth and her living mosaic. She is hopeful for our future, but as always it depends on our actions.

Please choose wisely and well for all our sakes.

CONTENTS

The Natural World

Human Beliefs

Epilogue

PACHAMAMA TALES

THE WATERLILY

Pachamama was in a quandary. She had two beautiful daughters: the sun Inti and the moon Killa. She had never introduced them to each other and feared they might be jealous.

Pachamama sat on a large lily pad thinking. Tortugita, a very old and wise soft shelled turtle, surfaced and looked at Pachamama. Pachamama explained her dilemma and Tortugita said, "I will talk to them."

That night just before dusk Tortugita resurfaced carrying an elegant water lily on her back. Inti the sun saw the beautiful lily and wanted it. Tortugita explained, "Inti, if you would like to see this flower every day, then it must be cared for at night while you are resting. I have spoken with the new moon Killa and she too would like this flower, but understands it needs your golden light as well. If you and Killa will care for it together – you during the day and Killa at night - I will give it to you to share."

And that is why we see the water lily open in the day under the sun's watchful eye, and close at night under the moon's silvery beams.

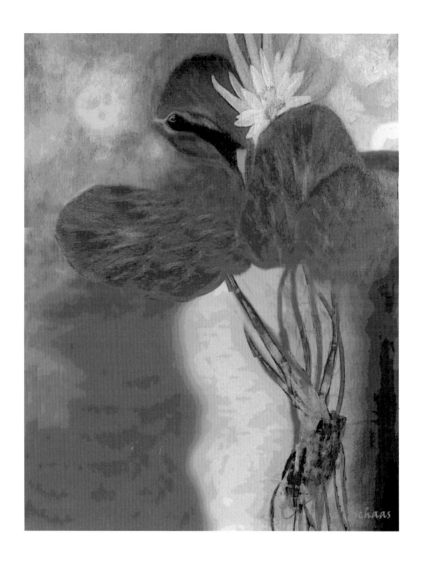

FIREFLIES

When the moon first hatched, Pachamama saw her crying. She held her close and asked, "Killa, what makes you so sad?" Killa replied, "Pachamama, I miss the light of my sister sun Inti."

Pachamama thought for a moment and then waved her hand over the gentle stream. Slowly water droplets drifted aloft, glowing with a soft yellow light, they sprouted wings.

Killa laughed. Pachamama said, "These little suns are fireflies. They are from your sister to remind you of her love for you, even in the dark."

And that is why we see fireflies at night.

THE NEW EARTH

Long, long ago, Raven decided he wanted a new earth. He thought and thought about it and finally went to Pachamama.

"Pachamama," he said, "I think we should get a new earth. This one has been badly treated – the air and water are no longer sweet and many are starving and thirsty."

Pachamama advised, "You must talk to Brother Frog." So Raven flew down and found Brother Frog. When Brother Frog heard Raven's request, he dove to the bottom of the lake and grabbed the largest glob of mud he could hold.

When he got to the surface, Raven was waiting and Brother Frog began to push the mud up to Raven. As he pushed, the glob became rounder and rounder. As the water dripped away, the sun baked the mud until it had a strong outer cover. Raven picked it up in his beak and flew toward the sky.

As Raven dropped the earth, the celestial winds blew it into orbit around the sun.

BABY SLOTH

Pachamama smiled down at Perezito her little three-toed sloth. She carefully helped it into a Secropia tree. It started climbing slowly to the top, stopping now and again to munch on a particularly delicious leaf.

As it climbed, Pachamama whispered, "Perezito, remember you are the steward of this tree and other trees that you use." Perezito barely nodded.

But after spending the day safely tucked away in its leafy sanctuary, he climbed down to relieve himself in a hole he dug at the base of its tree.

As the tree fed and sheltered Perezito so in turn Perezito provided nutrition to his trees.

THE EARTH SPIRIT TREE

Long ago when the world was new, Pachamama created the earth spirit tree. It stood very tall and strong and its roots ran to the center of the earth. For many years it grew until finally you could see the ends of the earth from its topmost branches.

It was about that time that Pachamama decided to create a great river that would flow all the way to the sea.

She asked the anacondas for their tears and those became the river's source. She further asked the anacondas to cry once a year to insure that the river kept flowing. And thus the great Amazon River was born.

But sometimes the anacondas' yearly tears flooded the dry lands and endangered the jungle animals. So Pachamama asked the earth spirit tree to provide refuge to the jungle animals during the anacondas' crying season.

If we are observant, we find the same complex relationships between water, plants, and animals in all living systems.

GREY RIVER DOLPHINS

Pachamama was very pleased with her great Amazon river. But she wanted to be sure that all of the creatures who depended on its waters were well cared for. So she asked the chattiest of her riverine flyers the Pygmy Kingfisher to be its custodian.

The little kingfisher took her job very seriously. She spent many hours flying over the river, talking with its inhabitants about their needs and reporting back to Pachamama. However, the river's dark waters prevented her from checking on creatures that lived below the surface. Pachamama told the kingfisher, "I will find you a water diver who loves the river as much as we do."

Within days, kingfisher was drawn to splashing in the water. When she flew over to investigate, she spotted the grey river dolphins, cavorting through the waters. They were very good gossips and they made Pachamama laugh. Kingfisher didn't think they were serious enough, but they did bring important news of the unseen dark water life to Pachamama.

HOW THE TOUCAN GOT ITS BILL

Toucan was not a happy bird. While he appeared boisterous and bright, he was very sad inside. But Pachamama got word of his sadness and stopped to see him. "Toucanito, whatever is the matter?" she questioned.

"It's my bill - it's so big and dark. I have wonderful jokes and stories to tell but everyone is afraid of me. They hide when they see me coming. "

Pachamama thought for a moment and then said, "Close your eyes, Toucanito, and I will help you." As he closed his eyes, a gentle rain fell on him. He felt the sun warming his feathers and a soft zephyr wind playing around his bill. After several minutes, the rain stopped and Pachamama told him to open his eyes.

He stared down at his beak and his eyes filled with tears of delight. Pachamama had used the zephyr to paint the rainbow on his bill.

From then on, everyone came from far and near to hear his stories.

SEA WOLVES

One day Pachamama was sitting on an ice flow contemplating the vastness of the blue ocean when she noticed the dorsal fin of a killer whale. As she watched, the fin came closer and closer until the head of a great orca rested at her feet.

She looked at the great orca and said, "My son, I see you have lived a great many seasons. Are you tired?" The orca replied, "Pachamama, I am very old and soon will be gone. I have heard all of the sounds of the ocean, but I would very much like to hear the songs of the pines before I go."

Pachamama pondered the orca's request for some time. Finally she said, "You are my greatest hunter in the sea, and I can change you into the greatest hunter within the pines, if that is what you truly desire. Your eyes and your coat will reflect the blue of your origins. But your end days will be on land for you can never return to the sea."

And so the orca was changed. And that is how the blue-eyed wolves came to be.

IRIS

Pachamama spent a long time designing the vegetation of the earth. Tall red trees, small green sprouts, blue berries, purple fruits - Pachamama drew them all using the living colors of the rainbow. And thus all she drew came to life.

One day, Pachamama accidentally dropped her brush and a stem suddenly appeared surrounded by long pointed leaves.

Immediately the leaves started murmuring, "What's our name? What's our color?" Pachamama glanced at her palette of colors. As she painted yellow on the top of the stem, she said, "Your name is iris, and although your color now is yellow for the sun, you can choose any color of the rainbow when you bloom for the first time." And that is why we see iris in a spectrum of colors.

HOW THE LIZARD GOT HIS THROAT FAN

One day when Pachmama was looking at her garden, she spied one of her newest creations - a small brown lizard.

"Brother Lizard," she said, "how do you like your home?" The lizard bobbed his head up and down and said, "It is truly magnificent, Pachamama - I am never hungry with all the wonderful bugs to eat and can change the hue of my skin quickly to match my surroundings which is terrifically helpful for hiding, but I have one very big problem."
 "Oh," she replied, "what is that?"
" I have no way to find females or to warn off other males from my favorite haunts because I blend so well no one sees me."

Pachamama thought for a moment and then gently touched his throat. The lizard felt a tingling and when he raised his head, an elegant fan expanded from his throat. In striking colors of red and orange, the extended fan drew attention. But it could also be swiftly hidden when danger was about. He knew it was the perfect signaling device for him.

And this is how the lizard got his throat fan.

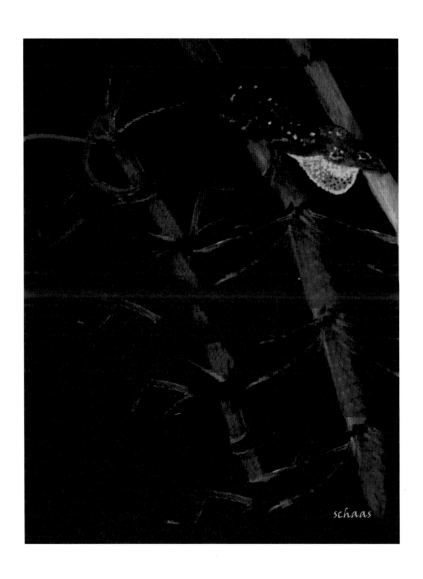

PACHAMAMA'S FIRST HELPER

Pachamama looked out on her vast living earth and decided she needed help. She needed curators to keep track of her animals and her plants and to tell her when she needed to modify her living mosaic.

It is said that she looked far and wide before she found her first curator sitting on a rock playing his flute. "Brother Flute Player," Pachamama began, "I am looking for someone to help me care for my world. It must be someone of goodwill, a healer, a lover of life, a teller of tales, and a belly full of laugher." Backflipping off his rock, the Flute Player bowed deeply and said, "Pachamama, they call me Kokopelli and I have been waiting for you."

And so it was that Kokopelli began his life-long service as a curator to Pachamama. In truth, he often caused Pachamama headaches from his unending pranks and foolishness, but he also brought great laughter to the world. And as we know that gift is sometimes in very short supply.

KOKOPELLI SERENADES RAVEN

For many months, male raven wooed female raven, but it seemed she had no interest in starting a family. She much preferred spiraling effortlessly aloft on the thermal updrafts. From high above the canyon she could see to the ends of the earth. Why give that up? Finally in desperation, male raven talked to Pachamama.

Pachamama listened as raven recounted his plight. She realized how much the female raven treasured her freedom, but also knew that unless young ravens were hatched there would only ever be one pair of ravens. She called Kokopelli, the flute player.

She convinced Kokopelli that he must play his magical flute music to entice female raven to lay eggs and raise her young.

Kokopelli waited until female raven landed on a very high point and then played a magical melody. Soon the two ravens had built a nest and female laid her first eggs.

FROG PITCHERS

Long ago Pachamama created bogs with nutrient poor, soggy soils. Then she thought about species that might thrive there.

The first plant she added was the carnivorous pitcher plant. Lured by nectar, insects landed on the opening and often fell in. The bottom of the pitcher held a concoction of rain water and plant chemicals which dissolved insects into a nutritious soup. Satisfied with her design, Pachamama moved on.

One day, Pachamama returned to see how her bog was progressing. To her concern, she found frogs sitting at the tops of the pitchers. She quickly called all the frogs together. "This is very dangerous," she began, "if you fall in you won't get out." "But Pachamama," the chorus of frog voices chanted, "we are very careful to stay at the top and catch the bugs so they can't get out. Every day we throw one down so the plants are never hungry either."

Pachamama talked to the pitcher plants and they agreed that the frogs should stay. And that is why we have frog pitchers...

schaas

WATER BEETLE CREATES EARTH

Long ago when the first peoples came to the earth, Pachamama helped them create their belief systems.

The ancestors of the Cherokee bands of the eastern United States spoke of a watery world where all of the animals lived above a sky arch. After a time, it became very crowded. But looking down, they could see no solid land. Finally, the little water beetle came down from the sky realm. Darting here and there, he could find no place to rest. Finally he dove down to the bottom and brought up some mud. The mud expanded in all directions to become the land we call earth and home to the waiting animals.

EPILOGUE

And so we come to the end of the Pachamama tales.
This does not mean there will not be future tales,
just no more to tell in our current place in time.

73576125R10022

Made in the USA
Middletown, DE
16 May 2018